KNOC

CW00428536

SPECIAL THANKS...

To mark turning 30, I wanted to publish 30 jokes that held the potential to help others beyond my own capabilities. In joining forces with talented illustrator Andy Tharagonnet, you're now able to hold this dream in paperback!

Andy, you've brought the life to my baby, the music to my party and your support means the absolute world.

Having dedicated my career as a PT to the promotion of health and fitness, diabetes is something I understand sparks increasing concern and requires vital ongoing funding. My grandmother 'Granny Mac' has battled with type 1 diabetes for over 50 years and her journey and management throughout my Grandad's recent passing has been simply inspiring.

She is soon to turn 90 yrs old and this book and with it, your donation to the world's leading charitable funder of type 1 diabetes research is my gift to her and everyone whom the charity supports throughout their own journey and battles ahead.

Let's go spread the love, tell a joke & make someone smile today... thank YOU for your support!

WHAT DOES IT TAKE TO MAKE AN OCTOPUS LOL?

10 TICKLES

What bear has no teeth?

A gummy bear

What's Forrest Gump's password?

1forrest1

WHAT DO YOU CALL A SLEEPING T-REX?

A DINO-SNORE

What do you call a guy with a rubber toe?

Roberto!

WHAT VEGETABLE FILLS EVERY SAILOR WITH DREAD?

LEEKS

Did you hear about the restaurant on the moon?

Great food, no atmosphere!

WHY SHOULDN'T YOU TRUST STAIRS?
BECAUSE THEY'RE ALWAYS UP TO SOMETHING!

What do you call a pig who knows karate?

pork chop

WHY COULDN'T THE LEOPARD PLAY HIDE AND SEEK?

BECAUSE HE WAS ALWAYS SPOTTED

**what did the
sushi roll say
to the bumblebee?**

- wasabi!

WHAT DO YOU CALL A FAKE NOODLE?

IMPASTA

WHAT DO YOU CALL A COW ON A TRAMPOLINE?

WHY is CINDERELLA SO BAD AT FOOTBALL?

BECAUSE HER **COACH WAS A PUMPKIN**

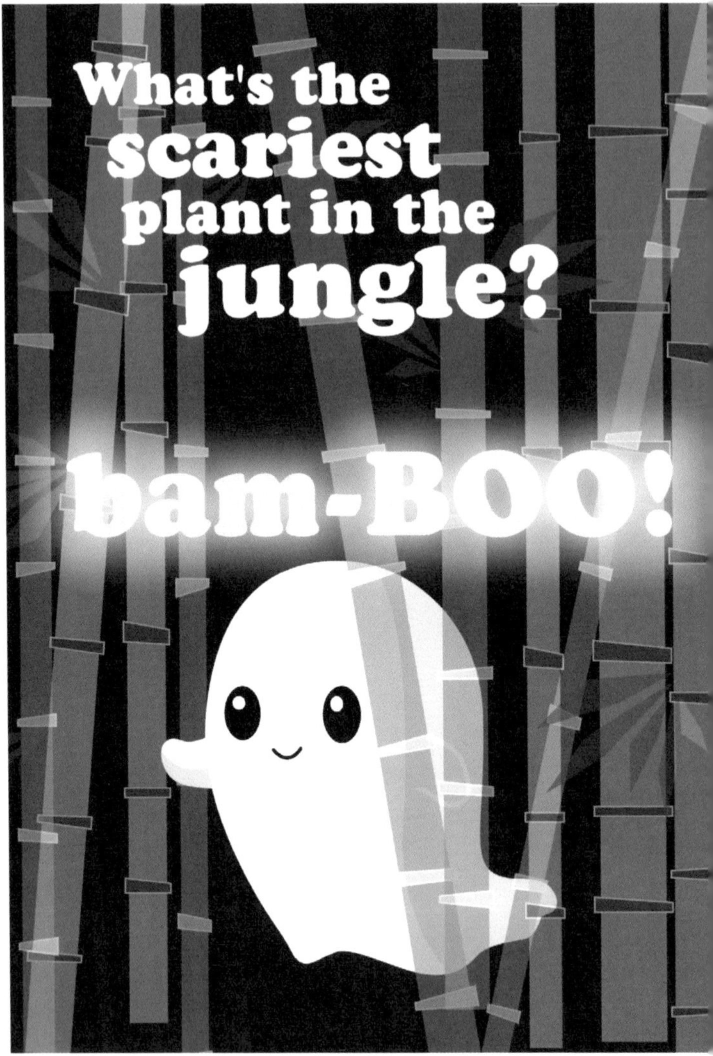
What's the scariest plant in the jungle?
bam-BOO!

what do elves listen to in the workshop?

w-rap music

What do you call
a singing laptop?

Adele

DOCTOR DOCTOR, THERE'S A STEERING WHEEL IN MY PANTS

IT'S DRIVING ME NUTS!

WHY ARE DEMONS AND GHOULS ALWAYS TOGETHER?

BECAUSE DEMONS ARE A GHOUL'S BEST FRIEND

WHAT DID
ONE FIREFLY
SAY TO THE
OTHER?

YOU
GLOW
GIRL

HOW DO YOU MAKE A TISSUE DANCE?

PUT A LIL BOOGIE IN IT

WHAT WAS THE WORLDS BEST DENTIST AWARDED?

A LITTLE PLAQUE

WHAT DO YOU GET IF
YOU CROSS A VAMPIRE
WITH A SNOWMAN?

FROSTBITE

I LOVE YOU
GRANNY MAC,

HAPPY 90TH
BIRTHDAY

DUCKY
X

JOKES

Tom Macnally

returnofthemac_nally

www.firststepfitness.co.uk

iLLUSTRATioNS

Andy Tharagonnet

mr_lina

www.andytharagonnet.com

Printed in Great Britain
by Amazon